The Secret of Santa's Songbird
African American Cover Edition

by
D. S. Jackson

The Secret of Santa's Songbird
African American Cover Edition

Poem Copyright © 2002 by D. S. Jackson
Book Publication Copyright © 2013 by D. S. Jackson
1st Edition

Cover Illustration and Design by: Robert Sauber
www.RobertSauber.com

ISBN-13: 978-1499175066
ISBN-10: 149917506X

Book Website
www.santassongbird.com
Email: DS@SantasSongbird.com

Printed in the United States of America

Dedication:

Heart
To
Heart

Chipper the songbird
hatched early one spring,

To discover that life
is a wondrous thing.

He wanted to see
the whole world from the sky,

So he sat in his nest
growing feathers to fly.

The wind swept his hillside tree
upward and down,

As he stood watching over
his old country town.

He heard children singing
and watched them at play,

And gathered such gifts
in his heart every day.

Spring turned to Summer
and Summer to Fall.

He grew splendid feathers
but this was not all.

Chipper had taken
to singing at night,

And each time he did,
he lit up like a light.

A gift of the kind
only heaven can send,

Had come from above
with a heavenly friend.

Other birds said,
"Chipper's ways are not right,"

"No night singing birds,
turning on and off light!"

Flocking and squawking
they called Chipper "strange".

They said he should live
outside normal bird range.

Then starlings forced
Chipper to fly away north,

Just as the chill
of the winter came forth.

Chipper flew many hours
to be safe and free.

He stopped for a rest
on an evergreen tree.

Below him a town square
was fully in view.

And people were doing things
festive and new.

The Spirit of Christmas
was traveling round,

In kindness and faith,
in sights and in sound.

Chipper was twinkling,
thrilled by the view.

The Spirit came to him,
and onward he flew.

He flew to the realm
where angels sing,

To hear from the giver
of every good thing.

Then one special song
was placed in his heart.

Earthbound he returned,
to continue his part.

Chipper arrived
in a most sacred place,

A caroling light
for a child of true grace.

Then onward he traveled
timing his way,

To sing on the Eve
of each Christmas day.

On the deep starry night
it became Christmas Eve,

Santa Claus had a snack
and got ready to leave.

He was shrink loading toys,
in his usual way,

When a ball of red light
appeared over his sleigh.

Chipper glided to Santa
while singing a greeting.

And Santa applauded
the light show and tweeting.

"Well now," Santa said,
holding out a gloved hand,

"What brings you tonight
to snow covered land?"

"May I go with you Santa,
to see-see-see?"

Chipper persuaded
and hopped cheerfully.

"I will stay sitting tight,
singing carols all night!"

"Ho-Ho!" Santa laughed,
"Yes, Chipper alright!"

So up they soared
into the sky,

And Chipper learned
how reindeer fly.

He saw the way
the night stands still,

Upon the timeless winds
until ...

Down from the winds
the reindeer flew.

The night grew colder
and the sky dark blue.

Chipper sang with a shiver
and Santa said, "Oh,

I think I will take you
inside when I go!"

Once the sleigh landed
upon the first roof,

Santa loaded his sack
with a magical poof.

Chipper chose Santa's hat
as a perch for the ride,

And the magic of Christmas
swept them inside.

The house was all warm
and sparkling with light.

Decorations of holiday
charm lit the night.

A tree full of ornaments,
each placed with care,

Gave the scent of fresh evergreen
to the night air.

Santa pulled from his pocket
a birdseed cookie.

He placed it with Chipper
up high on the tree.

Chipper ate every seed
then started to call,

A song of sweet dreams,
he caroled to all.

Everyone sleeping,
dreamed even sweeter,

Touched by the song
of this holiday tweeter.

Dreams filled
with favorite candies and toys,

Wrapped in the wonder
of Christmas day joys.

Santa bounced to the tune
in his merry elf way,

While placing the gifts,
to be found the next day.

Then Chipper asked,
"Santa, is song a gift too?"

And Santa realized
just what Chipper could do.

"Oh Yes!" replied Santa,
"the gift that you bring,

Will secretly echo
in all birds that sing.

All hearts you sing to
will feel renewed cheer,

Each time a bird sings,
any time of the year."

Chipper expressed
the full thrill of his joy!

He swooped round the room
like a spiraling toy.

Santa laughed as he gently
took matters in hand.

He motioned to Chipper
to settle and land.

"Now, my dear songbird,
onward we go!"

And back in the sleigh
they arrived all aglow.

On Santa's command
the deer leaped into flight,

And the sleigh lifted off
in a glorious light.

They traveled the world
by the Christmas Eve moon,

Like a song on the wind
bringing life back in tune.

Sharing love and great joy,
peace and good will,

As all who are giving
are sharing these still.

And when their grand journey
came to an end,

Chipper found a new home
with Santa, his friend.

"May the Spirit of Christmas,
bring peace and insight,

Merry Christmas to all,
and birdsong to delight."

Sometimes a gift comes,
as something we hear.

A new kind of wonderful
soon becomes clear.

And a treasure arrives,
in a whisper that brings,

A gift like the song,
a wild bird sings.

CPSIA information can be obtained at www.ICGtesting.com
Printed in the USA
LVOW10s1716071215

465787LV00021B/1346/P